One Gecko, Two Mynahs and More

Written by TODD E. SHELLY
Illustrated by ETHEL M. VILLALOBOS

Dedicated to

EMMA AND MIRANDA
and to the memory of
ABUELITA TEN-TEN

Published and distributed by

ISLAND HERITAGE
PUBLISHING
A DIVISION OF THE MADDEN CORPORATION

99-880 IWAENA STREET, AIEA, HAWAII 96701-3202
PHONE: (808) 487-7299 • FAX: (808) 488-2279
E-MAIL: HAWAII4U @ PIXI.COM

ISBN #0-89610-298-X
First Edition, Third Printing–1999

One Gecko,
Two Mynahs
and More

Written by Todd E. Shelly
Illustrated by Ethel M. Villalobos

ISLAND HERITAGE

One gecko serving curry and rice.

Two mynahs eating blue shave ice.

Three monk seals lounging by the pool.

Four fat pigs trying to be cool.

Five mongooses snorkeling in the bay.

Six booby birds going out to play.

Seven 'i'iwi taking in the sights.

Eight chameleons flying fancy kites.

Nine stilts showing off their leis.

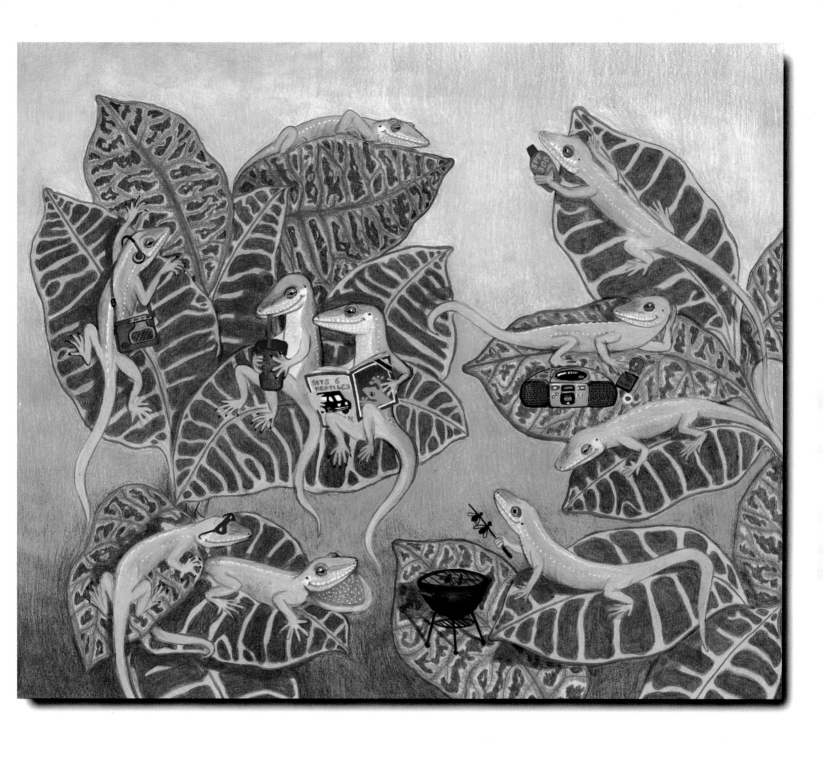

Ten anoles enjoying sunny days.

Eleven nēnē shopping at the mall.

Twelve wise pueo chanting "That's all."

GLOSSARY

GECKO – Geckos are nocturnal insectivorous lizards with large toe pads. Several species have been introduced to the Hawaiian islands, but probably the best known is the "barking gecko" so named because of its loud barking laugh. Geckos are considered good luck, as are the ceramic Japanese cats found in many of the local stores and shown in the drawing.

MYNAH – A common urban bird, mynahs were introduced to Hawaii from India in 1865. They eat insects and live in pairs. The mynah shown here is eating shave ice, a snow cone favored by island children.

MONK SEAL – These native seals live mostly on the tiny islands and atolls northwest of the main Hawaiian islands, although they are occasionally spotted in more populated areas. They feed mainly on fish and squid. Monk seals are very rare and are considered endangered.

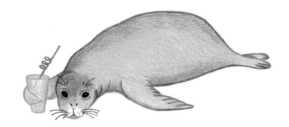

WILD PIG – Pigs were introduced to Hawaii in two waves, first by the Polynesians and then more recently by European colonists. Although pigs were intended to be domestic animals raised for food, some escaped and established wild populations. Wild pigs pose one of the biggest threats to native forests, because they uproot plants, damage their seedlings, and create light gaps where weedy, exotic plants can outcompete more shade-loving native plants.

MONGOOSE – The mongoose in Hawaii is the Small Indian Mongoose, which occurs over much of southern Asia. These mongooses are omnivorous and eat a variety of rodents, birds, insects, and some vegetation. These animals were introduced to the Big Island in 1883 to control rats and sugar cane pests. Unfortunately, mongooses were unsuccessful as pest control agents but have had a severe negative impact on populations of native birds.

BOOBY BIRD – Booby birds are very large sea birds that feed on fish. Booby birds do not sit and incubate their eggs like most birds. Instead they use their broad, webbed feet to keep their eggs warm. Both the male and female help raise the young. The three species of booby birds found in Hawaii and shown in the "Six Booby Birds" illustration are: the red-footed booby, brown booby, and masked booby.

'I'IWI – This spectacular bird is a native honey-creeper found in the upper canopy of high elevation forests. Its long, curved beak is used for collecting nectar from blossoms of the native 'ōhi'a tree, the red flower shown in the "Seven 'I'iwi" picture. Ancient Hawaiians used 'i'iwi feathers extensively in making ceremonial garb.

CHAMELEON – Jackson chameleons were introduced as pets but are now found wild in forests. They are a threat to native insects that evolved without risk from such predators. Only male possess large horns on their faces. The chameleons shown in the "Eight Chameleons" illustration are taking advantage of the strong trade winds near Sandy Beach on Oahu. One kite features the state fish of Hawaii, the humuhumu-nukunuku-ā-pua'a.

HAWAIIAN STILT – These tall, slender wading birds are found around marshy areas and mud flats and feed on fish, crabs and worms. Unlike many other native animals, these birds have adapted well to man's presence, and a large population persists near the Marine base on Windward Oahu. The birds in the "Nine Stilts" drawing are wearing leis, or floral garlands, which are commonly given as a token of affection or gratitude in the islands.

ANOLE – The green anole lizard became established on Oahu in 1950 from the release of pet store animals. Anoles are insectivores that are active during the day. They can change their color from green to brown, gray or tan to match their background. If grabbed, the tail may detach, allowing the animal to escape.

NĒNĒ – Unlike other geese that live near water, the Hawaiian goose has adapted to a terrestrial lifestyle and inhabits volcanic slopes on the Big Island and Maui. The nēnē nests on the ground, making the eggs vulnerable to introduced predators such as rats and mongooses. Captive breeding efforts were necessary to save this endangered bird. The nēnē has a vegetarian diet, which includes the native 'ōhelo berry.

PUEO – The Hawaiian owl occurs on all main islands but is most abundant on Kaua'i and Maui, especially in Haleakala crater. The pueo hunts by day and by night and nests on the ground in grass. In old Hawaiian stories, the pueo was revered as a guardian spirit, who was called on in times of danger and fear.

ALOHA